Hidden

Nathalie M.L. Römer

HIDDEN

Emerentsia Publications
Marielundsvägen 9c
711 95 Gusselby
Sweden
emerentsiabooks.com

Ordering Information:
Orders by U.S. trade bookstores and wholesalers. Please contact Ingram: One Ingram Blvd., La Vergne, TN 37086 • 615.793.5000 or visit www.ingramcontent.com.

Independently printed as a Swedish publication.
Interior design and layout by Emerentsia Publications.

Official Website:
nathaliemlromer.com

Official Facebook Page:
facebook.com/nathaliemlromer

Official Twitter Account:
twitter.com/nmlromer

HIDDEN

For my loving partner Anders.

HIDDEN

Chapter 1

KAYLA STARES THROUGH THE LETTERBOX to check if she sees her best friend of more than a decade, moving through the house.

"Kelly--I know you're in there. Hurry up already with opening the door. I'm freezing my *butt* off. I think the workmen outside are glaring at it *too*."

Kayla looks over her shoulder to glance at the men who are conspicuous in their attempt to stand in just the right spot to look at Kayla. She answers their attempts with a resolute middle finger. The men laugh.

"Fuck off!" she shouts, then, turning to the door once more, she pleads, "Kelly."

"I'm coming…"

Kayla frowns when her friend's voice sounds dull, almost like opening the front door is a chore suddenly, and almost like she doesn't even want to see her friend at all.

Kayla straightens up and looks somewhat perplexed at the door in front of her, then eyeing the window next to the door, she sticks her hand with the middle finger in a definitive upward position aimed to her right.

"You cunts can *go* now--" Kayla shouts and she scowls at them a moment later, then turns her face towards the door when she hears the door being unlocked hastily.

"About time," she states, pushing the door to give herself the chance to get inside, as well as stopping Kelly from closing it. "I was freezing my butt off here."

Kayla bends sideways and again sticks up her finger to ensure that those, outside, were forever reminded of her displeasure.

"Can you *not* do that?"

Kayla stares at the door. Kelly stands there hiding behind the door, "Are you okay?"

"I will be when you stop being so rude to them. I live here, and I have to deal with them after you've gone home."

"Oh, sorry. Why are you hiding like that? I thought you would want to go to the coffee shop before we have to go the last few lectures before summer starts."

"I don't feel up to going out."

"Why not?"

"I just don't want to, okay?"

"Sorry. Anyway, it's cold out here. Can I come in?"

"I guess so."

Kayla frowns for a moment at the lack of enthusiasm in her friend's voice. "What's up? You sound like you lost your mojo."

"I just don't feel up to talking today, okay?" Kelly spits out.

"Sorry, I just thought I could ask why you look so unhappy. I thought we were friends and could talk about anything."

"We can, just *not* about this. Please respect me for having some stuff I can't talk about."

"So…I guess you want to hide in your house and even from your best friend…"

"You guessed right. It's better *this* stays hidden from everyone."

Kelly closes the front door softly and walks to the

living room with her friend in tow.

She sighs and looks away towards the kitchen. "Do you want a coffee?" she asks.

"Sure."

"Go find something to watch and I'll sort it out."

Kayla stares after her friend for a few moments before she walks to the large sofa in the corner of the living room.

The abrupt clanking sounds from the kitchen tell volumes about the mood of her friend, causing Kayla to be a bit hesitant to sit down on the sofa. She glances through the window, thinking over what to say to convince her friend to go to the coffee shop after all.

Kelly is looking as pristine as usual with her hair done up, carefully applied make-up and her best top, like she was going out perhaps.

But she looked extremely sad when she opened the door. I wonder what's up with her. I hope she isn't being evicted by the landlord or something like that...

~~~

KELLY IS ALSO PENSIVE, LEANING AGAINST THE FRIDGE and thinking deeply. She knows her day is only going to get worse, especially if Kayla forces her to go to
~~~

university today of all days. She looks at the letter lying beside the sink. The news it told her wasn't the sort of news she wanted.

I guess I have to tell her she's the only one off to uni in August, she thinks bitterly. *Why the fuck did she have to turn up at all? I wanted a day alone for once--*

"Do you want sugar in your coffee?" Kelly calls out.

"Yes, one teaspoon, please," the answer comes a moment later.

"Want biscuits?"

"Sure…"

Kelly walks into the living room holding two huge mugs, steam rising from each, and with two packs of biscuits under her arm.

She hands one mug to Kayla who finally sits down, maybe a bit awkwardly since she'd been caught out having this behaviour after the earlier brashness towards the workmen outside.

"So, why no uni?" Kayla asks.

"I don't feel up to going?"

"I guess we can skip it for a day. Now I think about it too I don't want to go either. Those girls from yesterday were too annoying in my opinion…"

"What girls?"

"The ones who asked us to come to that graduation party they're organising."

"I wasn't paying attention."

"I noticed. Well, they wanted both of us to *go*. They kept hammering on about how pretty you looked and that shit."

"Oh, those girls. I switched off because they started talking about my appearance. You know *both* our moms always tell us not to pay attention to it. To be more into what's up here…"

Kelly taps her forehead.

"Yeah, yeah, I know…So, have you decided what you're going to study next year?"

Kelly pauses for a few minutes with her answer, masking the action by drinking several sips from her coffee. She speaks hesitantly, "No, I'm still deciding…"

"Fair enough. I guess you have all your options open unlike some of us…"

"What do you mean?"

"Nothing. Just saying…"

Kelly stares at her friend for a few moments then turns away and stares pensively out of the window. The 'many options' so aptly indicated were so few. Even fewer if she included the other bad news she'd received.

What's the point of having friends, being smart, supposedly being pretty - according to those friends at least, or having to make out you're perfectly happy? Kelly ponders, *it won't help me at all when she of all people discovers the news. How much can I tell her? I better tell her before--*

"Are you going to tell me why you're here…other than to pester me about this *thing* you want to do?" Kelly snaps.

"Can't I visit a friend suddenly?" Kayla asks.

"Of course, you can. But please, don't pester me about the graduation party, okay?"

"Sure thing. I guess I can go alone *if* needed."

Kelly grunts at the response, then she pretends she didn't hear the implied suggestion in the wording.

I guess she does want me to go. Perhaps one last time to see that damned place before I leave for good. Best to leave without telling her or to say anything to Mom either. Neither of them would understand why I left so suddenly. I guess I will miss this friendship…

Chapter 2

KAYLA FROWNS AS SHE LISTENS CLOSELY to her friend.

Kayla has her own reasons to feel annoyed for having to visit, and it was mostly caused by her mother dragging her from her warm bed.

She complained about not wanting to go out.

She has things she's hiding from her friend just as much as she's now suspecting her friend is hiding from her.

"I guess we can talk about uni. Just not about whether I'm going," Kelly says softly. "So, who do you think is going to the party?"

"Lizzie and her sister are going. I overheard them talking about what dresses they were going to wear for the party and almost arguing about it too," Kayla answers. "I saw them from the bus on the way here. They were in that shop I pointed out to you. I saw Lizzie from the bus and frankly…the dress she chose was butt ugly."

Kelly laughs suddenly. "Is it the flowery one? The one you said you wouldn't mind as a summer dress?"

"Until I saw it on Lizzie, I hadn't considered how massive the flowers are on it. Nope. It's off my list now…"

"So, what are you wearing instead?"

"This…"

Kayla picks up her bag, opens it, and pulls from it a white plastic bag. From it, she lifts two garments; one deep purple, the other dark red.

"I know you said you don't want to go. Consider this a gift. Sort of also a way to say sorry for snapping at you just now. You can use it for…whatever you decide."

Kayla hands the red garment to Kelly.

"I think the colour goes with your hair colour. I chose purple because you know how I am with all things purple…"

Kelly smirks.

"I think mom still regrets going shopping with us five years ago when she won that shopping spree. We ended up with so much purple for you, and red for me, that day…That was a nice day."

"I guess that's when your love for clothes started. Is that a new top, because I can't recall seeing it before today?"

"I got it from a catalogue…"

"Which one?"

Kayla glances around the room.

"A new one. It arrived last month. I had some spare money, so I splurged a bit."

"Since when do you buy from catalogues?"

"Since I don't want to go to shops all the time. I prefer being home without crowds around me."

"Oh, right. I guess seeing Lizzie made me realise I don't like it much either. Any chance I can look in the catalogue?"

"It's in the drawer of my desk in the room next door…"

"You always have everything in that desk. Are you hiding something in it that allows for that?"

Kelly laughs. "Do you think I'm like her…The

Doctor. I'm not even into that sort of television shows as you should know."

"Anyway, can I look at the catalogue to see if it has some shoes to go with this dress?"

"Sure, go get it. You know where the desk is…Want more coffee?"

"Yes, please."

Kayla gets up and walks off to get the catalogue. At the same time, Kelly picks up the two mugs and walks back into the kitchen where she places the mugs on the worktop then leans forward sighing deeply. She glances at the paper lying there beside her.

What the fuck am I going to do about this? I'm certain she's going to accuse me of doing stuff to get rid of her as a friend. And that wouldn't be true. I want Kayla as a friend. But I cannot stay here because of the news I received--

A noise in the hallway interrupts Kelly's thoughts for a moment.

I guess K and K may go to pots over this shit.

Kelly remembers the precise day when the idea for 'K and K' had started.

Both had been waiting at the doctor's practice for an appointment. They waved at one another when their mothers started to chat.

It was when they walked off for food from the vending machine in the corridor that they exchanged names.

Both had giggled when they realised how closely their names resembled one another. Then, Kayla suggested the whole 'K and K' thing and she'd gone along willingly. *But now it feels so ridiculous to keep using it. We're adults. I guess I'll just have to confront it when I go back into the living room.*

She turns on the kettle to heat the water and quickly prepares each mug with coffee granules, sugar, and milk when she hears the drawer of her desk slam shut.

"I found it…" Kayla shouts out.

"The coffee is ready too," Kelly calls back while she pours water into each mug. "I'll be there shortly."

After placing the mugs on the table, Kelly sits down opposite her friend, and after waiting for a moment for her to speak, she picks up one of the biscuits and dunks it into her coffee.

"Yuck! Do you still do that?"

"I like it that way…"

"Your choice. I think it ruins the flavour of those

biscuits. But anyway… I think I found the perfect pair of shoes in this catalogue. How do you order this stuff?"

"There's information about it on the last page. If you download their app you can order your shoes immediately using your card."

"Ah, right. I guess I'll do that then…"

"Scan the QR code on the first page. That will install the app on your phone."

Kelly sips from her coffee while watching her friend complying with the instructions.

She decides to omit that using the app also earns her a commission.

More spending money for me, and she won't even know it.

She briefly smiles and stares out of the window for a while, listening to Kayla's muttering.

I guess I can't blame her for wanting to go to the ceremony. It's not like she has much chance for party time as it is…

"So, what's up with you?" Kayla asks quietly. "And don't give me the crap about not wanting to talk because I know you too well. In the end, you always tell me everything…"

"I guess I have to tell. I received a letter about something I hoped that I wouldn't--" Kelly pauses for a sip then continues. "If you're so nosey about it, go check it. It's in the kitchen."

Kayla is about say something further, but from the corner of her eye, Kelly sees her forcibly restraining herself, then mouthing what's obviously a swear word. She then gets up and silently walks off.

Kelly looks back out of the window, now waiting for the tirade that will come from the kitchen when the news in the letter becomes known to Kayla.

I guess I'll have to explain all of it now. Mom doesn't even know yet. I guess by tomorrow everyone in my family and hers will know…

Chapter 3

KAYLA STOMPS BACK INTO THE LIVING ROOM with the dreaded letter in her fist, and before she drops down on the sofa, she glares at Kelly.

"So, when were you telling me, then?" Kayla shouts. "Was I just going to turn up some day and find this house empty? Fuck you for forgetting we are supposed to be best friends."

"Sorry…" Kelly whispers, feeling somewhat sheepish for a moment.

"Well, maybe you need to remember it more often as you never seem to call me any more," Kayla snaps. "You never visit me either, forcing me to come across town to here…"

"Since when is that a problem?" Kelly says quietly, averting her gaze away from her friend.

"I guess you're avoiding a discussion about this. I can tell something is up…"

"It's nothing…"

"And all this stuff about *you* not wanting to talk. When we're at uni you always talked so much. Right now, you have said so little," Kayla says. "You really worry me."

"If I've not been around much, neither have you actually."

Kelly picks up Kayla's phone from the table and flips through the call log.

"Let's see when you called me last…" Kelly looks up and she smirks at her friend for several minutes before she continues speaking, "It seems you've only called me four times in the last three weeks. I see eight missed calls from me, three from my mom, and five from your mom here. Explain *that* to me?"

"I guess I didn't want to talk to them. But I didn't realise you'd called me so often…"

"I didn't either." Kelly grins a moment.

"I guess I called because I wanted to talk. But the fact you didn't answer tells me a lot."

Kayla looks down, unable to explain the reason suddenly; unable to tell her friend she has her own issues just like her friend seemingly has.

"I guess I can be as grouchy as you if all you're going to do is snap at me and bite my head off."

Kelly drops the phone back down on the table, and Kayla immediately picks it up and places it in her bag.

There's a long silence before Kayla decides to broach the earlier topic, "I guess it's still a 'no' in terms of going to the ceremony?"

"Okay, it's a maybe. It depends on stuff…okay?"

Kayla nods, but Kelly sees her eyes are glazed over now.

I wonder what's she is so upset about--

Kelly's thoughts are interrupted by the sobs coming from across the room. She looks up sharply and frowns a moment.

Then, another audible sob.

Her frown deepens for a moment then she glances away quickly before Kayla notices her stare at her. The sobs remind her of an incident when they were both around ten years old.

Kayla had gone off to the park with a few of the neighbouring friends. It was only weeks earlier that they'd truly become best friends. When she arrived, she found the other kids standing in a circle around Kayla;

all taunting her. Kayla was crying and occasionally would scream to be left alone.

I think it was my fist in the face of that boy that sealed our loyalty for life, Kelly thinks.

Kayla had a cut knee and a bruise on her arm. She never told her what had happened exactly, but afterwards, it was like a little bit of the spark that had attracted them as friends - while they waited in the doctor's office - had gone from her.

She still doesn't have that spark. I guess that day affected me too, in a way. I've always been so protective of her, almost like we're sisters instead of friends.

The other incident Kelly remembers that affected Kayla terribly, was when her parents had split up for several years. Though five years later they did move back in, it seems Kayla's relationship with both her parents, was screwed up in a very odd way.

Especially with her mother, it seems. They were close when we first met. But now they hardly talk. And I've noticed that she always hides it whenever things go bad in her life somehow - like when she broke up with Alex.

Kelly sighs and looks in her cup. Though she wants another cup of coffee she doesn't feel up to asking Kayla if she wants one too. So instead, she places her cup down on the table then pulls her legs up, so she sits in a tight ball. For ten minutes, it's silent.

Kelly waits for the sobs to lessen then completely stop.

Then, she speaks gingerly, "It seems to me we're both in a foul mood today. We must talk. We cannot ignore whatever is eating us up. You don't cry so readily these days. And I--" She stops speaking, swallows hard, then adds softly, "I have something I need to tell you too. But first, I want to know what's up with you. You seemed to act like a bitch on my doorstep when those men decided to catcall you, but now you seem a different person totally."

"It's nothing..." Kayla whispers, her voice being drowned out by an audible sob that in other circumstances would have caused Kelly to laugh. But she stares firmly at her friend. This time, she isn't going to dodge the issue that seems to have arisen between them.

"Tell me, Kayla," she says sharply, causing an angry stare. She repeats the words once more.

"I guess I feel bad still because of Alex. I saw him the other day with this other girl and--" Another sob escapes Kayla's mouth. "And he was laughing with her like he never did with me. I'm certain he saw me because he seemed to whisper in her ear, and then they both laughed. She purposely kissed him on his lips after that..."

"Do you know the girl?"

"It's--" Another sob. "It's Lisa…"

"You mean that *bitch* who used to bully you?"

"The same…"

"I see. I guess she could do with her nose punched like that boy…"

"No…you can't do that. It will cause issues for me. She works five doors down the road from where I work. I have to walk past the shop where she works."

"I guess a beating is off the menu," Kelly says. "How about you get another boyfriend?"

"Who do you have in mind?" Kayla asks softly and somewhat hesitantly. "I don't want to end up with someone else who'll be like Alex and have another Lisa to come along and steal *that* boyfriend from me."

"It won't happen. I will make sure of it."

"You don't know how it is to think that you're properly in love and think that the relationship is going strong, and then he dumps you. I've never seen you with any guy…"

"I don't have time for any sort of relationship with a guy at the moment," Kelly snaps harshly.

"Why not?"

"I don't want to talk about that, okay."

Chapter 4

KAYLA STARES AT KELLY INCREDULOUSLY, then she laughs hysterically.

"So, you think I can somehow walk in *your* shoes all of a sudden? Be popular with plenty of friends like you? I am not pretty enough, and Alex dumping me proves it."

"His loss, not yours. You are smarter than I am, and you know it. You can be a scientist after uni…"

"Who would date a scientist…" Kayla grunts.

"Someone will…"

"I doubt it."

"Someone *will*," Kelly repeats as she reaches for the mugs and the letter.

"Want more? I guess we're going to make ourselves

hyper on this coffee today…"

Kayla nods curtly, then stares at the garden outside.

She's watched a moment longer before Kelly gets up and walks to the kitchen once more.

She places the mugs on the worktop and the letter beside them then glances up when she sees someone pass her window.

As she pushes the curtain aside, she sees it's one of the workmen pulling a cable of some sort. She drops the curtain when he blows a kiss towards her.

Dammit, I wish they would be gone by now. No wonder Kayla was so peeved with them.

Kelly looks at the letter one more time then places it on top of the fridge for the moment, meaning Kayla won't see it unless she noses around the kitchen.

"Kayla are you hungry for some proper food?" she calls out.

"Errr, yeah, sure…"

"Come to help me with cutting veg, and we make our spaghetti omelette."

"Aren't we fifteen years too old for that?"

"Naah. It was always fun to eat it when we were young, and it still is…"

Kelly turns when Kayla arrives in the kitchen.

"Time for us to embrace our perverted childhood, before we sit down and have some serious talk, okay?"

She gets a nod in response.

"I think we got everything in the fridge. If not, we'll improvise," Kelly continues. "Which type of pasta do you want? There is macaroni, and a wholemeal pasta I bought at last market day, and I found this other pasta that supposedly tastes spicy."

"Let's try the last one."

"Okay."

"We're missing cottage cheese for the filling," Kayla comments.

"I have a cream cheese on the top shelf that might work."

"Found it…"

While Kayla gets to work on cutting the vegetables, Kelly prepares the pan for the omelette and fills a pan with water for the pasta.

"Have you had this pasta before?" Kayla asks.

"Yeah, a few days ago. It's delicious…I guess I'm addicted to it."

"Good."

They smile at one another for a moment; for a moment forgetting their bickering and perhaps also each of their worries.

"So, as you've decided to start to play cupid for me, who did you have in mind as a boyfriend for me?"

Kelly giggles.

"So, I guess you do want a boyfriend," she says. "What about the earlier talk about scientists never getting one?"

"I guess you're right about me finding someone else. I just need some 'me' time first…"

"Sure. We don't find your dream boy in a day. Maybe…hmm…I have an idea."

"Oh no, now I'm scared…"

"I guess *none* of them idiots outside qualifies as a dream boy, right?"

"Nooo, how dare you even suggest that. They're butt

ugly. All of them."

"And none of them will know how to keep up with you when you're a scientist."

"Phew…"

Kelly pauses the conversation to prepare the pasta further.

When Kelly turns once more, her mind has shifted back to her earlier thoughts of childhood.

"You said Alex, and yes we have to talk about it, was with Lisa. If I recall she was the one who pushed you down in the park when we were kids. *Tell* me what happened back then…"

Kayla is silent for several minutes before she strains an answer.

"She claimed that I had short hair because I'm gay and that I had a thing for you…"

"So what if you have short hair. *Not* every person with short hair is gay."

Kayla looks up, surprised at the response. She'd expected a rebuttal or an outburst of anger, but *not* an answer that made it out that it's okay to have short hair for other reasons.

She said that for a reason. Why?

"Did anything else happen back then?" Kelly continues, seemingly ignoring her own comment.

Kayla, however, decides to confront the issue.

"Are you saying that being gay is fine with you? Not that I am…"

"I know you're not gay. You have too much of a wandering eye when it comes to the boners whenever we're at any nightclub."

Kayla laughs.

"Oh, right. I see…And is that why you know you can find me a new boyfriend?"

Kelly nods.

"When we're out and about I'll just check which boner you stare at the longest, then force you to go chat up that guy. As I said, it's very easy to get you a new boyfriend. You did check Alex's boner before he became your boyfriend?"

Kayla shakes her head, feeling her face go red.

"So, Lisa is now stuck with a loser with no ability to make boners…right?" Kelly says plainly before she turns and picks up the pan containing the pasta and drains it.

She turns on the heat under the frying pan before she turns and asks, "Is the veg ready?"

Kayla nods absentmindedly, then mumbles, "Maybe he pretended to like me…"

"That's the spirit," Kelly says. "Now you realise he was always a loser. I don't know if you remember, but he was one of those standing around you in the park and laughing like all the others. Maybe he just pretended; to find another way to tease you. But what he thinks doesn't matter anymore."

"So, he might have planned it with Lisa?"

"He might have been her boyfriend for a lot longer than when you saw them together, thought of that?"

"Errr…no."

"But as I said, it doesn't matter. What matters now is that you move on, start over, whatever…"

"Okay…"

The silence between Kelly and Kayla is just broken up by the chatting and laughter coming from the workmen in the street just beyond the kitchen window. It's obvious each of them, by their soft giggles, this is the cause of their amusement over what the men are talking about.

HIDDEN

When a few minutes after they hear a joke, loudly shouted out by the man who'd been catcalling Kayla, it causes both of them to roll their eyes.

~~~

BUT KELLY IGNORES THE HESITATION she hears in her friend's voice. She turns to busy herself with the advancing frying process of the vegetables, while it seems Kayla decides to prepare the omelette mixture without her asking to do this.

Kelly knows she's aware of the preparation process.

After a few minutes of frying, Kelly adds the pasta to the mixture and then, as she turns, she changes the topic for a moment to something else said by Kayla.

Something that makes it more obvious to her to tell her friend what's going on with herself…
~~~

Chapter 5

KAYLA LOOKS UP WHEN HER FRIEND TURNS once more; she's surprised when her normally talkative friend doesn't immediately speak.

She sees an uncommon worry flash over her face. Kayla decides not to say anything, which is unusual for her as well, remembering what her friend had said just before.

She wants me to remember what she said. She does have a point, though. I have things I have to tell her, but it seems she's trying to tell me something too…

"So, what do you want to talk about?" Kayla asks. "I can tell you want to tell me something, so if you want to play cupid for me, can we also talk about you as well…?"

"For a start, you need to get that notion that I'm popular out of your head," Kelly snaps. "I was in the toilets…in a cubicle, when some 'friends' walk in. I heard every word they said. I actually understand how you feel a lot better than you realise…"

"Oh, right. So, what's up with you, then?" Kayla says, somewhat hesitantly.

"First, we sort out whatever the hell is going on with you," Kelly counters. "First off, why the hell, were you so rude to them? I know they catcalled, but still…"

"I said sorry…"

"You did, but it doesn't explain why you behaved in that way."

"So why the comment about you supposedly not being popular?" Kayla states, sighing deeply, then diverting from the conversation, she points at the pan. "I think our omelette is starting to burn…"

"Shit!"

Kelly grunts as she listens to the laughter coming from her friend. Though, after a time, she also thought of her responses as funny, because she had almost forgotten about the omelette.

"Most of the omelette is edible still," she comments as she picks up two plates and brings them to the table.

She sits down, sighing deeply. She looks pensively at her friend, considering carefully her next words, "I think what I'm trying to say is that there's something you're not telling me. Something about the way you behaved as you arrived is… off… that's the only way I can describe it without being rude."

"You said you wanted to discuss things. You said we'd talk about other stuff before I had to tell you."

Kelly looks sharply at her friend. Her voice has sounded so pained suddenly.

"What's wrong? Tell me…" she says, holding her hand over Kayla's hand firmly like she always did in the past whenever she had to tell something that Kayla might not like.

Her question is only met with silence, and with Kayla picking at her omelette with the fork in her other hand.

"Let's just eat," Kelly says softly. "We will talk after…"

The meal is eaten in silence, both of them caught up in their own thoughts for a while.

~~~

KAYLA FLOPS DOWN ON THE SOFA, and a few minutes later, she's joined by Kelly who pulls herself into a ball. They stare at one another for a few minutes.

"Now what?" Kayla asks.
~~~

"Well, I guess you need to explain what happened as a child," Kelly answers. "You never wanted to tell me. But I think it's linked to what happened in the park…"

"I have to admit I took it hard when my parents split up," Kayla whispers. "I always wondered if they would split up again after they got together again."

"Do you know why they split up?"

Kayla shakes her head.

"I guess you need to confront them some day and ask. But let's first make sure you're in a good place."

The encouraging comment is met by a weak smile.

"The medication does make it tough to feel positive," Kayla admits.

"What medicine?"

Kayla reaches for her bag, and after rummaging for a few minutes, she pulls out a small, white bag she unzips and then tumbles the contents in between them.

Kelly picks up two of the bottles, reads the label, then frowns a moment and looks at Kayla.

"I'm no expert, but this is powerful stuff? How long have you been taking them?"

"This one is a three-week treatment my doctor put me on ten days ago. She says it would help with my mood swings. I shouldn't take it for longer than that. Any longer than three weeks and it will actually affect me in a negative way."

"What are these other meds?"

"This one is what I've taken for the last *three* years. It helps to keep me in a positive place," Kayla continues. "Those two together are supposed to improve me considerably, and the doctor claims that going for a trip might actually be even better. She says that being in a different environment other than at home with my parents, or even this city, for that matter, will make me better and less likely to need the meds…"

"Do you want to go on a trip?"

Kayla nods, saying nothing now.

"If you had a chance for a trip, would you want to go?"

Kayla nods once more.

Kelly looks away a moment; silent again. She's now pensive over her situation, especially how much she should tell.

"Do they help you?" she asks when she notices

continued silence.

She glances back at her friend inquisitively.

She's met with a nod.

"Most days they do, but there are also bad days," Kayla answers after a minute more of silence.

"I guess that's true for any illness or whatever mental health issue a person might have," Kelly suggests. "You're a graduate with a medical degree, but I don't need their use explained to me as I can guess what these medications do…"

"I want to be *off* them in two years from now. I read that being on them for more than five years is bad for a person. After that, it can be addictive," Kayla explains. "Maybe we should do something useful with our degrees. You have a food science degree; I have a medical degree. Could we research and find a way for people with depression to eating in a certain way, so they rely less on pumping chemicals like those in these medicines…"

Kayla lifts one of the containers and shakes it right in front of Kelly's face.

"Okay, you don't have to emphasise your words by annoying me…" Kelly blurts out.

Kayla giggles for a few moments. "But am I *right* in

what I'm saying about food somehow being helpful for people like me?" she asks, sounding serious again.

"In a way, yes…"

"In what way?"

"Well, we're supposed to eat a healthy diet--" Kelly looks incredulous when Kayla laughs so uncontrollably that she flops sideways on the sofa.

"Did I say something funny?"

"Yes, you did…really, really funny…" Kayla says between more giggles.

Kelly frowns, then snaps forcefully, "What did I say that's supposedly funny, huh?"

"We're supposed to eat a healthy diet…" Kayla imitates Kayla's voice before she laughs even more.

"You what?"

"Is a spaghetti omelette healthy?" Kayla asks, smirking now teasingly at her friend.

Chapter 6

KELLY WAITS FOR KAYLA TO STOP LAUGHING as well before she speaks again. "I guess I'm contradicting myself when I do half-burned spaghetti omelettes," Kelly says, smiling broadly. "But we're allowed to indulge our foodie needs from time to time…"

"Half-burned food is hardly indulging it…"

"True, but I guess I was distracted by our conversation," Kelly says. "But let's get back to what we were talking about…You said the bullying started that day?"

"Pretty much," Kayla answers quickly. "I do remember Alex standing by and watching it happen. Lisa was joining in with the taunts and name calling. She was going on about my short hair, saying I looked like a boy and that I would never have a boyfriend because of it. It was horrible…"

"So now you're convinced Alex was just pretending

to like you?" Kelly asks.

"I don't know any more. I guess I've decided to convince myself of it…"

"Maybe he *did* have genuine feelings for you, but maybe it's Lisa who decided to be mean again…"

"I guess so. I never liked Lisa much…"

"Neither have I. She even tried to insinuate herself in the group of people I hang out with whenever we were studying for our degree," Kelly says. "She wasn't even studying food science, then tried to tell us stuff that all of us knew was totally wrong. She made a total *ass* of herself with some of them."

"Did Jo graduate?"

"She did."

"Good! From what I overheard she also deals with depression," Kayla says. "I think she could be included in our effort to try to make stuff better."

"Do you know how to get a hold of her?"

"I have her on my Facebook friend list. She sent me a friend request a few months ago."

"Okay, I guess she found you on my friend list."

"Maybe we need to start one of those groups, and call it… errr… Maybe we can use K and K in some good way, like perhaps making it a group where like-minded people, so in the end we'd be helping more people than just you and me. I'm sure that whatever you're going to tell me is as important as what I've been telling you. But I'll respect your wishes and will tell you what happened to me first…"

~~~

KELLY SITS DOWN OPPOSITE HER FRIEND after she'd retrieved a bottle of cola to share. She places a bowl of ice cubes and two glasses beside the bottle. Kayla divides up the ice cubes then opens the bottle and pours them both a glass full of the cold drink.

"I guess we need to figure out how to sort out things. Both of us…" Kayla says finally. "I'll tell you what happened. I guess it's time for it…"

Kelly nods silently.

"They were making claims about you, saying you were only friends with me because--" Kayla stops speaking a moment and speaking quieter she adds, "… they thought you and I were lesbians. That *you* were only interested in me for that reason, and that me with my short hair was interested in you for that reason."

Kayla looks for a reaction from Kelly.
~~~

"Go on…" is her only comment before sipping from her cola.

"I'm *not* gay, if that's what you're worried about, Kelly."

"I know you're not. You cannot stop staring at guys, even if you were blindfolded."

"The reason for my short hair is because it just doesn't want to grow fast. It never has… It does save me a lot in hair dresser bills. How do you keep your hair so nice anyway? Oh, never mind, let me continue…"

"Anyway, when you arrived that day, they'd just told me to stop being friends with you or that somehow I'd regret it. In fact, it was Lisa who said it. I guess I kept that hidden from you."

"I guess you *were* worried when I turned up."

"They suggested that you'd join in with their teasing. When you didn't, I was surprised. But then felt ashamed for not telling you immediately about what had happened."

"Remember what my mother told *us* when she lost her job? She said that sometimes things happen that you cannot prevent, but it's how you act afterwards that defines who you become. In a way, you became the compassionate person I wanted to *be* friends with because of that day. Haven't you ever thought of it in that way?"

"Honestly, no… actually. I only ever thought of it in a negative way."

"I guess that's caused by your depression, and perhaps, those meds…"

Kayla glances sideways at the containers lying on the sofa beside her. "I guess you're right…" she comments. "Maybe I need to stop taking them sooner…"

"Don't stop abruptly, though, but I agree. They may be contributing to how you think about stuff."

"Maybe I can skip one day every four days initially, and if the way I feel is different in a good way, then I skip one day ever three days, then ever two days, and then take it every other day."

"That sounds about right." Kelly nods curtly. "And remember that feeling positive got my mother her next job that she still has now. She even got a raise and a promotion a few months ago. It proves to me that a positive outlook can do wonders…"

"Oh…I didn't know about it. Congrats with that…"

"I guess…*if* you kept in touch more you'd know. I even shared the news on Facebook. You didn't see it?"

"Errr no…sorry. When did it happen?"

"I posted it three months ago."

"I was giving Facebook a miss at the time. So much bad news appeared on my news feed that it affected me…errr…"

"I can understand the reason. So, it's okay…"

Kayla nods, then pauses before speaking once more. "I guess I should pay more attention to your Facebook page at least…"

"And keep in touch more on *that*…" Kelly nods at Kayla's phone lying on the sofa beside her friend.

"I will from now on. I promise…"

Kelly smiles warmly at her friend before she sips again from her drink while she thinks a new happy thought, *we're talking now about the things that drove us apart for the last year or so. I guess we needed to talk in this way because it forces both us to admit to the feelings tearing us apart. But I need to keep her talking…*

Kelly sighs, hoping that it's not noticed. But it becomes clear by the mumbles coming from her friend that she is trying to figure out what to tell next.

The words, when they come, make Kelly jump and almost spill her cola over her top.

Chapter 7

KAYLA HAS OBVIOUSLY WEIGHED UP the conversation as it continued and decided to be blunt.

"Are you trying to hide your own illness from me? Are you telling me you're depressed too?"

"I don't want to talk about it yet. I will tell you. I'm just trying to figure out how to tell you, okay?" The answer is voiced very hesitantly.

Kayla frowns when Kelly seems to plead with her eyes, she nods and adds, "I'll finish my story. *When* I'm done, you tell me yours…"

Kelly nods, swallowing hard now because now she was committed to a promise made.

"So, I was telling you about that day in the park…" Kayla continues, speaking softly. "When I got home my parents were angry about my clothes being scuffed. And then they argued later about me after I was sent to my bed… I actually remember it so well as I was told I couldn't have any desserts for a week."

"Them arguing about your clothes being scuffed is a bit much…"

"Yeah, I know. I still don't know why they argued…" Kayla whispers. "I never dared to ask them…"

"Hmm, interesting."

"Why?"

"Because it proves to me that your parents were already having issues long before that day," Kelly explains. "Do you remember Mitch? It was the year we went to middle school. He was in our class up to that year, then the following year he was gone."

"Yeah, I remember."

"I heard from someone that he went to live somewhere else with his father. His sister supposedly lives with her mother," Kelly explains. "According to Ricky, who told me all this… Mitch apparently didn't want to live with his mother because of something she'd said about his father. Ricky wasn't sure what but claims that his mother made a claim that his father slept around. According to him, Mitch then discovered his mother with another man so is certain that the facts had been twisted by her. His sister didn't want to believe it…"

"I doubt either of my parents was having an affair…"

"Maybe not, but they *did* live apart for five years, right?"

"Hmm, you have a point," Kayla frowns. "Now I wonder even more what was really going on."

"Okay, what I'm going to explain now isn't directly related to this, but in food science, we were taught something specific that's relevant to this situation," Kelly continues. "Although, in my opinion, it was the most boring part of the studies."

Kelly pauses to think for a moment.

"We had lectures about packaging, and colour of food. The suggestion that Professor Thompson had given during the lecture is that colour influences us. For example, that's likely why this label is so bright red…" Kelly points at the bottle in front of her.

"So, I'm wondering if, in a similar way, there something about behaviour about-- Let me think for a moment to explain this in the correct way…"

Kayla nods.

After a few minutes, Kelly continues. "I think the scuffing has a different meaning for each of your parents," she says. "If something happened where either of them caused an event, and the scuffing simply reminded them of it."

"It makes sense to me…"

"Can you remind me of how long they were married before you arrived?"

"Six years. Mom always claims I was…how did she put it…oh yeah, I was 'unexpected'," Kayla answers. "But she always seems sad when she says it."

"She was the one who left…" Kelly states quietly, then adds, "Similar to Mitch almost… His father left, your mother left."

"My dad was grumpy afterwards…"

"Hmm, was your relationship okay with him?"

"We never really talked about her leaving us. Then, five years later, she just turned up out of the blue and moved back in with us, and Dad never even questioned why she came back," Kayla answers. "When I tried to ask either of them, they were blaming me for the split instead of explaining. Each of them said that when I asked. I never told the other parent that I asked the same question and I got the same answer from them both…"

"That's horrible. It wasn't your fault for *them* to have problems with their marriage…" Kelly says. "But anyway, back to my explanation.”

After waiting for a nod from Kayla the explanation continues, “As I said, packaging and the colour of packaging influences us. For example, green is often associated with nature, birth and renewal…”

“Kind of what’s taught in medical science. A change in colour can indicate something wrong with a person.”

“In any case, you caused something to appear different from the norm they were used to,” Kelly states, now staring directly at her friend. “You may not have caused the different situation, but you did influence it. They unfairly punished you for their own idiotic behaviour by blaming you…”

“So, me thinking for a decade that it was all my fault is stupid…” Kayla states matter of fact, without a hit of upset or anger in her voice. “I guess I need to put the blame where it’s due; with them and then let them deal with it…”

“Let me get the worksheet we were given. It will show you how the marketing shit is involved with the things we were being taught. When you see the graph, it makes more sense…”

“Okay.”

Kelly gets up and quickly walks to her bedroom and after just a few minutes is back with a bundle of paperwork. She flops down on the sofa beside Kayla.

"Let me find it quickly…" she mumbles.

Kayla stares at the paperwork that seemingly represents years of study. When finally, her friend finds a single sheet of paper she's handed, and she stares at several graphs with photos beside them, recognising her friend's handwriting.

"As I said, I think you want to look it almost like a cause and an effect…like in this graph," Kelly explains. "As you see, the graph shows that the 'attraction' becomes greater the more colourful the packaging is. If the cola bottle was brown, people wouldn't go for it."

"What has this to do with my parents being annoyed over my scuffed clothing?"

"Nothing directly. But it's the behaviour they showed that interests me," Kelly counters. "I think you reminded them of something that happened. Attracted their attention to a bad experience without meaning to do so…"

"So, all I did was be like the red colour on the cola bottle…?"

"Sort of, yes. Okay, admittedly, this part of my degree wasn't my strong point. But I think there's a link between how people behave when certain colours are present. Why do you think I stick to wearing white tops with black of dark brown trousers?"

"Because you want to blend in…?"

"Exactly that. Now, remember what you wore that day?"

"The new bright red top I was wearing for the first time ever that day…"

"Red is a colour also associated with love, or in a negative context it's associated with lust…"

"Hmm, so by seeing my clothing smudged, it reminds them of something that happened before that day, which then causes them to fall out and separate for five years. I realise now what you mean…"

"Even though it's just a bunch of stupid talk trying to explain to you that you didn't cause their behaviour…"

Chapter 8

Kayla grabs hold of Kelly's hand and leans closer to her friend and stares hard at her. She grins suddenly when she sees the worry appear on her friend's face.

"Kelly, I know…" she says calmly. "I understand what you mean with this rambling on. You say it wasn't my fault. Even if you have an odd way of explaining it."

"I guess what I'm trying to say is that you want to pay attention to what they did or are doing, and *not* concentrate on your own behaviour as the cause…" Kelly quickly explains.

"Ah right, so I guess I should start to write down stuff I remember."

"I think that's a way to start to figure out things," Kelly says, pointing at her own writing.

"I'm crap at marketing. I still am, even with an

unexpectedly high score, but…I think in the end I figured it all out by writing things down. That's what I really wanted to tell you by showing this. The graphs are a small detail in all this mess. In a way, your memories are a mess too, and the possible cause is these meds…"

Kelly picks up the bottle which contains the pills that Kayla had referred to before as being addictive if taken too long.

"I'm no expert on medication, but if you take any medication long, it does mess with you," she continues. "At least, that's my opinion."

"That's why I want to be off them as soon as I can…" Kayla whispers, looking down.

"If you want to get better, you have to work hard at it," Kelly states firmly. "But usually it starts by admitting you need to fix something is the first step to fixing it."

"I don't want to talk to Alex…or my parents. Or anyone else I had to deal with for the last decade," Kayla says softly. "I think all of them are just contributing to how I deal with life. Like I saw said in a video on YouTube the other day…"

Kayla pauses and sighs deeply, "Too many people out there just don't take it seriously when someone says he or she is depressed," she continues. "Alex was always saying 'get over it already'…"

"Forget about Alex. If he didn't understand how you felt, he didn't deserve you…" Kelly says gently.

"I know, but it's so hard…" Kayla wails.

"I can tell you had real feelings for him…"

"I did. That's why it hurts me so much when he said he was splitting up with me, and then never even explained what the reason was for it," Kayla explains. "I didn't expect it to happen…"

Kayla lets out a sob.

"Then I saw him with Lisa, and my mind decided to tell me why…" she continues. "I guess all he saw was a loser who could not even control her emotions."

"You're *not* a loser…" Kelly squeezes Kayla hand tighter. "I have an odd way of explaining it, but one thing I don't need to explain, and that's about why I am your friend," she continues. "You're my friend, and I stick by my friends."

"I know…" Kayla whispers. "I wish I felt better than this…"

"Have you taken these today?"

Kayla shakes her head.

"My stomach feels bad today, so I don't want to take

any…"

"Let's make this the day off, as you had suggested earlier," Kelly suggests. "Then, you take these the rest of the week, and next Monday you have your *next* day off… How does that sound to you?"

"I guess I'm fine with it…"

"You can't be 'just fine' with it. You must deal with it. You can't keep *it* hidden anymore," Kelly says sternly. "Okay, I *did* have to go to extreme measures to get you to admit what's going on with you…"

"I guess I had to guess *that*…" Kayla says, grinning now. "You always did it too when we were kids. I guess you like to get to the solution with a curve in the middle of it…"

Kelly shrugs her shoulders and nods a few times, but she stays silent now in anticipation of what her friend may say next.

"So, do I continue with my story…?"

"Yes, please…" Kelly answers, speaking softly.

After Kelly has fetched a new bottle of cola, Kayla sighs before she speaks again. "I remember the evening when Mom left. I don't think I cried as much as that day at any time in my life," Kayla says quietly.

"She just left without any explanation?"

"Yep… and Dad never spoke about it either."

"Hmm, that's horrible really, considering how young you were at the time."

"I'm convinced now, after all your explanations, that they think they were being nice to me," Kayla continues. "But it all hurt so much…"

"I can hear in your voice that all of it still hurts…" Kelly comments. "But *if* you start talking about it, the pain will lessen. I promise…"

Kayla nods again, then she grabs the cola bottle and pours the drink in her glass she drinks down quickly before refilling the glass once more. She lets out a massive burp.

"Excuse me…" she says, going bright red.

Kelly collapses backwards, laughing loudly even if she's just laughing to dispel her unexpected nervousness suddenly overwhelming her. She glances sideways to check if it's noticed that she, too, hides something important. It's not…

Now I know about her problems I must make up for lost time. I must make sure she can be happy for once in her life.

Kelly considers her other options as well as to

whether she should even comply with her friend's wish to also tell what's going on.

My issues are tougher to deal with. She needs to be able to cope with knowing about it…

"Then, there's the stuff with Alex. I never really told you about how he and I ended up together," Kayla whispers. "When you found me in the park, he was there. I know I already told you that. It was a few months before he and I got together that I happen to bump into him in the street…literally."

Kelly grins because she remembers how clumsy Kayla always was as a child. She'd admitted to this fact enough times.

"He didn't recognise me immediately, but I did recognise him," Kayla continues. "I was a bit surprised as I'd heard he had moved to the other side of the country."

"I didn't know about that…"

"I didn't either. He claimed he had just arrived back in town. And he claimed he was pleased to see *me* of all people. When he asked for my number, I was stupid enough to give it to him. I guess I brought all that happened next to me on me by my own stupidity…"

"You're not stupid…"

"I *am* stupid…"

"No…you're NOT! Remember always that you're not stupid, not even because he did this to *you*…"

Chapter 9

KELLY CLAMPS BOTH HER HANDS OVER HER MOUTH.
She'd never yelled so loudly at her friend in all the time
they'd known one another.

"What the hell was that, Kelly? What are you so
angry about?"

Kelly looks away, her face going bright red. As an
answer, she shrugs her shoulders.

"Answer my question, or are you going to be a *bitch*
just like Lisa. I can go if that's the case…"

"That's not why I yelled…" Kelly whispers. "Sorry
about it. I have stuff on my mind, too. But I want to
help you first…"

"Oh, okay. So, when I'm guessing that--"

"I'm not gay. I'm also not having boyfriend issues.
Mom is fine. And I spoke with my dad last week, and

he's fine *too*…" Kelly quickly blurts out.

"Riiight…"

Kelly stares for a moment at her friend because it didn't sound like she was convinced by the answer she got. "I'll tell you later, okay…" she states. "I'm having a hard time figuring out how to tell even you about what's going on."

"Sounds tough, but okay. Shall I tell you what I saw Alex do last week?"

Kelly nods.

"As you know, he and Lisa are supposedly an item…" Kayla smirks suddenly with measured delight. "But I don't think he knows she's playing him for a fool. In a way, I can understand how he will feel if, suddenly, he would find himself out in the cold. There's no way I'm taking him back. You convinced me of that. Thanks for that, by the way…"

"So, you think Lisa is…?"

"I think I saw her kissing this other guy. I don't know who he is. He isn't from around here…"

Kelly flops back laughing loud. "So, while he decides to hurt you, he's being set up for being hurt himself?" she asks.

"I think so. And that's why all the sudden I'm not bothered about it any more."

"Riiight..." Kelly copies Kayla from moments before then Kelly and Kayla stare at one another.

Suddenly, both are in a heap of giggles like they might have been a decade earlier. Their giggling continues for several minutes before they can stop with the self-imposed amusement.

"I guess we can pretend to be kids again..." Kelly suggests. "Even if it's for a little while."

"Kelly, whatever it is you need to tell me, please remember that I'm your friend," Kayla continues. "Real friends stick together, no matter what happens. You always say that. Even months of us not speaking to one another ended up with us finding each other once again..."

"You're right. Now, are you going to tell me more about what you saw?"

"About seeing Lisa?"

"Yeah, because you made me damned curious," Kelly answers.

"I'm damned certain I saw them a week or so *after* I had broken up with Alex...after I saw them together-- kissing."

"It's likely she's messing around with many different guys. And hides it from each of them. Hurting others, like *you*--just as an easy example--in the process."

"I...I don't know. I just know I got hurt by him..." Kayla admits.

"Do you want to meet someone new?"

"I guess so..."

"Here or somewhere else?"

"Will it make a difference?"

"I think so. In another city, or whatever, no one knows either of us, and they can't hurt us with stuff from the past..."

"Are you suggesting you move *too*?"

Kelly nods.

"Uni is over and done with. *We* can get a job anywhere..."

"I guess we need to live in a city of some sort if I'm going to get the job that I want..."

"Or close to one..."

"Hmm, I guess that works too. Though I'd need to rethink options depending on where we end up. But it does feel odd to leave…"

"If you have a new environment around you, you might not need these eventually…" Kelly holds up the bottle with pills. "You've only used this for a short while, so you should be able to get off them easily."

Kelly doesn't notice Kayla's exact copy of her own behaviour, because she's suddenly as pensive as her friend.

They both look up when their discussion is interrupted by the rowdy laughter coming from outside.

"What the fuck is going on now?" Kelly mutters.

"I guess…errr…I guess they're talking about me… about us," Kayla whispers. "I guess they're making assumptions about us."

"Did you say anything to them before you knocked on my door?"

"Errr…I can't remember. Perhaps. Okay, they were rude to me, and I was in a bad mood, so I had a go at them, okay."

"Why?"

"Because--" Kayla begins saying but she stops

speaking for a moment, then blurts out, "I guess it's my mood that causes it. From being depressed…"

"I guess it's something we can't fix," Kelly says, sighing deeply. "I guess the only options open are for me to leave from this place *or* for them to be done with the work soon."

"What are they doing anyway?"

"Fixing the sewage pipes for the houses in this street. And they started with the damned work just last week."

"And for how long?"

"Until the end of this year…"

"Sheesh…Okay, sorry about me having a *go* at them. Had I known about that, I would have kept my mouth shut."

"There's option number *one* also, and that is what I have to talk about…"

"But we're not done talking about what's going on with *me*. A promise is a promise. Let me finish first, then you can tell everything going on with you. No more secrets. No more of this hiding stuff from each other. K and K never did that before so why start now…"

"Are you sure about that?"

Kayla nods curtly.

"Continue then…"

"Right, where was I?"

"Lisa… I think."

"Oh, yeah. The bitch really makes her rounds it seems because a day later I saw her in the arms of another guy…"

Kelly smirks then speaks again, "I could almost start saying she's a slut."

"I guess that's a good way to refer to her. But whatever she's up to, she's going to cause many conversations between two friends, like us, across the city. I'm not the only one with a broken heart…"

Chapter 10

Kayla stares at the cola bottle on the table as she waits for Kelly to finish on the phone. Her comment about Lisa had the opposite effect of what she'd expected her to do.

She didn't expect her friend to rush to the phone, and then spend the next hour calling every single person Lisa may have hurt with her actions.

But deep down, Kayla knows this is what makes her friend so popular.

She cares too much about the others around her.

Kayla looks up surprised when suddenly Kelly slams the phone down.

"Fucking bitch…" Kelly blurts out.

"What's wrong?"

"I think I know why she's doing this stuff. You're *not* going to like it…"

"Why not?"

"Because according to Rachel she's trying to take revenge on me for helping you in the park that day. Rachel claims she hates *me* for being popular…"

"Are you trying to say this is some sort of roundabout way of taking revenge on you? For helping me in the park that day?" Kayla squeals.

"I guess so…"

"How does Rachel know about it?"

"She's friends with Lisa's older sister. She mentioned Lisa."

"And she decided *not* to tell you for what reason?"

"Until I described the situation, she didn't realise who was involved…"

"And where does the part of me not liking this fit in?"

"Because Rachel mentioned that Lisa made a claim to *her* sister, and the claim is that *she* told everyone at uni you're gay and that you broke up with Alex because of it. She totally twisted the reason for the breakup on its head…"

"Fucking bitch."

"I can agree with *that* assessment…"

"What can we do about it, though?" Kayla throws her arms in the air to demonstrate her obvious despair.

"Not much… Anything either of us says now will just make it all worse," Kelly says wryly.

"I guess you're right."

"So, I guess we need to figure out what we can do about all this," Kelly continues.

"I don't how we can sort this. I'm fuming mad now about it, though," Kayla states. "I've had to deal with Lisa in so many ways that it's not even funny any more…"

"I didn't know that…"

"I guess I've been stupid enough to pay attention to her threats for far too long."

"But…we agreed no more secrets. So, whenever you're ready to tell you to have to tell me what she said to you, okay…"

Kayla nods then she looks down, blushing suddenly.

"I guess I never noticed because I have so many people trying to be a friend with me…" Kelly says softly. "I'm so sorry…"

"Why are you apologising to me? It's Lisa who should be apologising to both of us, and if ever Alex discovers he's being played like a fool by her, he better not come running back to me…"

Kelly laughs before speaking.

"So, I guess you're done with being bullied by the sound of it?"

"You're damned right. That bitch will get her just reward one day. *Not* from me. I'd want the chance to get away from here, and start somewhere fresh where no one knows me…"

"It could be a possibility…"

"How?"

"I guess I have to tell you what's going on with me to know why…"

"Now I'm really curious…"

"There is…errr…there's something going on with me. Something I need to fix."

"Oh, like *what*? You're perfect as it is. If by fixing you mean a boob job or something stupid like that then I'm not interested in knowing about it."

"It's not anything like that. It's…errr…"

"By the sounds of it, you're embarrassed to talk about whatever it is."

"You're not making it any easier…" Kelly yells.

"Sorry…No need to yell at me, okay…"

~~~

KAYLA GLARES AT KELLY, AND THEN SHE LOOKS AWAY once more. Silence had followed each of their outbursts in the last hour or so. Kayla realises that Kelly had almost told her what's on her mind or going with her if she hadn't made a stupid comment toward her.

It makes Kayla even more aware that the situation with Kelly might be more serious than she'd been assuming for most of the morning.

How will we even make it to the end of the day if we're being nasty towards one another? Kayla thinks bitterly. *We're supposed to be friends…*

"Lisa seems to really want friends to become the worst of enemies, don't you think, Kelly?" Kayla whispers. "If we don't talk things over, we're letting her
~~~

win…”

“You’re right,” Kelly whispers back. “I know you’re right. I’ve never had to deal with any of her bullyings, but right now, it feels like I might as well have been on the ground in the park with you…”

“Don’t say that. You’re what kept me from giving up.”

“I did?”

“Yes, and it may be the fact you got so popular that in a way also helped me from getting worse bullying from Lisa. It also helped me cope with what was going on with my parents. It stopped me falling to pieces, and perhaps stopped me from having stronger medication than this…”

Kayla lifts the container for her pills and rattles it for a moment, then suggests, “Whatever it is that goes on with you, you’ve given me the tools to help *you* with it… okay?”

Kelly stares at Kayla for several minutes, unable to speak and rather confused about how her friend seems so different.

“Okay…?” Kayla repeats the last word of her statement to try to elicit a reaction from Kelly. She’s met with more of her friend’s blank stare.

"What I mean to say is that you can tell me what's the matter with you afterwards. Before you do, I'm going to tell you what *my* plan is right now. I want to change my life to be better. Whatever it is you're dealing with, you can count on *me* to make certain you're going to go through alone. I've already guessed it's something painful, maybe sad and by your reactions I can tell you feel you'll hurt me with it. But nothing, I repeat, nothing will hurt me as much as being in the same room as Lisa and Alex. I can cope with what you need to tell me…"

Kayla takes a deep breath. "I guess I can finish my story *first* though…"

Chapter 11

KAYLA STARES AT HER FRIEND with as much determination she can find. Shy as she'd always been in direct confrontations, Kayla wants to be more like her friend. Kelly had said she's as smart, maybe even smarter than herself. She'd said that beauty comes from inside. And happiness. She knows that dealing with her depression head on and getting off the medication of more than a decade, will likely bring the happiness she so craves for.

"I *want* to be off these meds before I get involved with someone new. I've depended on them for way *too* long…"

"How long?"

Kayla is suddenly hesitant again, but not for long, "I think we need to make this a team effort. I help you with whatever you're going to tell me, and in turn, you can help me."

"It does depend on how long you've taken the meds. The longer it is, the tougher getting off them will be."

Kayla glances down towards the pill pot in her hands. Now came the part she'd never told her friend about. Admitting to something kept secret was tougher than she'd ever realised.

"I'm guessing from *your* reaction it's been a long while. When did you start taking them?" Kelly asks gently. "Just for your information, being depressed isn't--shouldn't--be something to feel ashamed about."

"I feel bad because I didn't confide in you sooner about how I feel...felt. Fuck, I never knew how tough it would be," Kayla whispers.

She looks up at Kelly then continues, "Do you realise there are people around who seem to think it's all just a game. According to their opinion, I'm like this to try put blame on others. That there are some who claim that I'm somehow making everything someone else's fault."

"I don't blame you for anything. It's *not* your fault you are ill in this way," Kelly states forcefully. "I've been a friend of yours for over a decade for one simple reason. I trust you. I believe in you, and *you* always believed, and still *do*, in the best in everyone. Life's a bitch, and it caused you to become this way. I don't like it when anyone acts like a bitch towards you so we're going to deal with this together. However hard it is... For both of us…"

Kayla smiles at her friend. A warm, genuine smile showing deep appreciation, then she speaks once more, "I'm guessing your issue is more recent because unlike me, you've always told me whenever things are on your mind."

"I guess I have to be true to those words then one more time. I have something I must tell you."

"What's wrong? I can tell from your voice it's something really serious."

Kelly reaches up and takes hold of her hair, then looks away for a moment before she turns to her friend and speaks softly. "I guess the chemo will get rid of this…"

Kayla sits upright, looking wide-eyed at her friend. "Did you just say what I think you said? No, please, not *that*…"

"It's true."

"That's way more serious than anything I'm going through right now."

"It's not as if I'll die. The doctors say they caught it very early. I will…errr…I'm going to be getting the treatment for three months. That's the reason why I'm taking time off from going to uni."

"I see… So, what will it involve?"

"Well, chemo first, then a long list of meds and some will be way more addictive than *that*."

Kelly points at the pill pot that Kayla decided to drop next to her on the sofa. Kayla looks at the container, then back at her friend. "What sort of meds?" she asks. "I know you probably already analysed what they do but I'm not like you in that way."

"I know what they'd do to me. But you can help too. In fact, if I'm not mistaken, there are types of food that are good in that they can help perk you up somewhat."

Kayla thinks about the suggestion a moment, then she nods.

"So, what we can do because of each of our education, is help other persons," Kelly continues. "Yes, I would have wanted to become a surgeon as I had told you a month ago, but then ten days ago I got the report from the doctor, and he suggests that after the chemo I need a long period of rest and nothing stressful. Hence why I had the idea for the trip I mentioned before."

"Ah, so that's the reason for it. Where were you planning to go?" Kayla asks quietly.

"I want to go on a trip to another country."

"Where?" Kayla looks hopeful at her friend.

"To Australia. And I'm *not* going for the beer or Bondi Beach. I want to go see kangaroos and koala bears. I know just the place…"

"Ah right. Yeah, that sounds like fun. And you want me to come along for the ride?"

"Of course…"

For a good ten minutes the room is awash with silence, with each person looking away, caught up in their own thoughts, then Kayla speaks up once more.

"So, *no* Bondi Beach for us?"

"Not until my hair grows back, and that may take a while."

"Can I go even if you can't? It's a place I've always wanted to visit one day."

"Of course. And perhaps letting your hair down while there and just giving yourself permission to have a whole day, more than one day even, of fun. It can help you immensely," Kelly suggests. "*When* I'm better I'd want to go there too. And I expect to be introduced to all the new friends you managed to make…okay?"

"Errr…okay." Kayla looks directly at her friend now and is met by one of Kelly's inviting smiles. She smiles back then looks around the room. "What are you planning to do with all your belongings while you're in Australia?"

"Most of it will be sold before I planned to leave. I'm having an open house tomorrow. I delivered over a hundred pamphlets through people's letterboxes in this neighbourhood last week. Do you remember Sammy from biology?"

Kayla nods.

"She's coming here with her boyfriend and his van. She's bought my wardrobe, also those three bookcases, and the spare sofa in the study. She's collecting them tomorrow. The rest of the furniture I'm hoping to sell during the open day tomorrow."

"So, I guess you'll need help with it."

"Only if you feel up to it."

Kayla considers the options for a few minutes, then nods hesitantly.

"Just do as much as you can cope with, and if not, you can always hide in my bedroom with your nose in a book."

Kayla grins a moment, then quietly says, "I guess I can play bookworm if needed."

"I bought a bunch of new books last week. I guess you'll find a book there to your liking."

Chapter 12

Kayla gets up and walks from the room speedily. "Just going to check what you're reading these days…" she calls out over her shoulder.

"Go ahead. You know where my bedroom is."

Kelly flops back in her chair, then sighs.

That went better than expected, she thinks, inwardly smiling. *Hopefully, I can help her…*

Kelly listens, and she can hear Kayla's muttering loudly.

I guess she didn't expect me to pick those books. It was quite fun to try to find good books all with the same title.

"Is everything okay, Kayla…Did you find the books?"

"Errr… yeah. I find it hilarious that you did this….

Why *did* you do it?"

"I found this Facebook group. They had a challenge going there."

"What challenge?" Kayla asks as she re-enters the room hoisting a stack of books in her arms.

"It was listed in a Facebook group I joined…it was…yes, it was about two months ago. The group is for authors and readers, and one of the authors posted the challenge, and it involved finding twenty books all with the same title."

"Sounds like fun. I should to try do the same." Kayla grins at her friend.

"Well, maybe if we're going to help you with your depression your task is to find twenty books all about positive things."

Kayla stops a moment before she sits down. Kelly looks at her and sees her friend is obviously contemplating the idea. She nods then sits down.

"I guess I could do that."

"The idea of it, as you'll see looking at the books I bought, is that they can never be by the same author, genre or trope."

"Maybe before we go on the trip, I could get some

books. I guess there's enough time to read the books while we travel to Australia."

Kelly nods.

"It will take a lot of organising…"

"I know," Kayla answers, before adding. "Is your chemo over there?"

"No, I'm doing it here before we'd go."

"Where?"

"In the city. They don't have the facilities at the local hospital," Kelly answers.

"Are you getting it done on your insurance?"

"Yes… luckily it's covered."

"Ah, right. Anyway, can I borrow *this* book?"

Kayla holds up a book, and Kelly grins broadly when she sees the book.

"And since when do you read erotica, huh?" Kayla asks, giggling now.

"Only since participating in the challenge," Kelly replies.

"Ohh…and since *when* do you read them?"

"Hmm, this one would be the *first*. Kitty sounds like a raunchy girl and the story is fun… I read the first chapter, okay."

"Maybe I should hold the book against the window?" Kayla says teasingly.

"Nooo…Don't you dare show that book to them," Kelly blurts out but the next moment she's laughing hysterically then she manages to compose herself, "It's too late anyway. The damned book fell out of my bag as I was opening my front door, and those workmen saw it."

"Is *that* why you were so sneaky opening the door?"

"I guess so…"

"How long have they been out there?"

"Three weeks already. They're rather an annoying lot. They make comments every time I go out to put my rubbish out. The neighbour noticed it, and now he'll knock on my door to find out to check if I have anything to take out, so I don't need to do it myself."

"Sounds like a good neighbour."

"He and his wife moved in only a month ago. I'll miss them when we go to Australia. But she's a nurse so said it's better for me. She said I had to stay out of the sun when it's the middle of the day."

"Even I know it's better to do that. But I do think that we're ending up with a tan both of us, eventually. I doubt anyone will recognise us after a few years living there, especially if we're going to be looking at kangaroos and koalas."

"Where I had to visit in Australia is close to a national park. Just two days of a bus ride from it. So, when I'm in a better shape, we can visit it."

"Sounds like a good plan."

Kelly nods, then she continues, "The destination I had planned is somewhere you'll enjoy a lot…"

"I will? Why so?"

"There are so many animals there…"

"Now I'm very curious."

"Auntie Josie lives in Australia…"

"You mean…?" Kayla squeals.

Kelly nods.

"The ranch with the animals is hers."

"Ah, right. Hmm, I read that being around animals is good for a person healing from illness. They say owning a dog is good for that…"

"Auntie Josie has a few dogs too. One of them is pregnant apparently. She said that when I got there, I can pick one of the puppies as mine. If you come too you can choose one too."

"Oh, cool. I never had any pets growing up…"

"I know, you silly, which is why I was not only suggesting for you coming with me but why I think *you* should choose a puppy too. To make up for lost time."

Okay, I guess the easy part is sorted. It sounds I'll have my best friend with me in Australia. But then there's the rest of and it relates to some of what she already told me.

"So, when we're going, we'll be staying with Auntie Josie?"

Kelly nods once more.

"She's sorting out the top floor of the barn. She was going to turn it into a guest house anyway but suggested we can test it out for a few months before we go on our trip around the country with her…"

"Doing what?"

"She's participating in a few exhibitions to show off

her animals to promote the work she does at the ranch. She runs a rescue sanctuary…"

"So, we'd have jobs?"

"Yes, well, not *me* initially, and it's optional for you. She said we can have a rent-free holiday courtesy of her *if* we're interested. But to be honest, I wasn't sure about it, so I said I'd think it over and discuss it with you."

"I think we should *go* for it. And yes, I'd work if needed…and…errr…"

"What's up?"

"I just thought of something. The lecturer at the university said I could earn extra credits for my degree if I wrote a good paper about food in the context of something. Maybe writing a paper about the food those animals eat might be the winning ticket to get those credits. It requires I have to do fifteen hours of work too, so if you *do* speak to Auntie Josie before we leave for Australia, can you ask her about it?"

"I certainly will do that. I'll give her a call later tonight, so it gives her a chance to be awake properly…"

"Oh yeah, it's a half day difference in time zone… Forgot that for a moment."

"I doubt I'd get a positive answer if I woke her up…"

"Very true…" But as she answers Kelly seems to look away and now appear to be pensive once more…

Chapter 13

KAYLA FROWNS, AND SHE NOW WONDERS what's really going on with her friend, because as the day progresses, it's becoming more and more obvious that she's struggling to tell something important.

If it's just that she's worried about cancer she needs not to worry. I think I understand why she was hesitant based on my own situation. But what else could be going on...?

She thinks for a while, observing Kelly. It seems to her now that the real reason of hesitation was still hiding another secret, another hidden revelation to be told. Kayla finally concludes she has to admit why she's having issues, and why she was hiding those feelings from Kelly.

"Kelly..."

No response.

"Kelly, I need to tell you how long I've been hiding

this depression from you," Kayla says softly. She opens her bag again, and she holds up a bottle of medication. "I've been on *these* for more than a decade. I was diagnosed with…I am dealing with depression, Kelly. It's hard to deal with it. It's tougher to explain how I feel. People always act oddly whenever I tell them I'm depressed, but I don't want you to think of me any different. I'm still that *same* person you said is your best friend…"

Kelly turns to stare at her friend, and her face is devoid of any emotion. She seems not to hear what's said to her. Kayla frowns then considers her next words carefully. She must try to find out what it is in the most tactful way she can find within herself.

"Did something happen with you and your parents?

A silent pause, but after a few minutes, Kayla sees Kelly shake her head.

"Kelly, tell me what's wrong," Kayla shouts out. "If I don't know I cannot help…"

"Remember what you said earlier about the park. How you told me nothing happened?" Kelly whispers.

Kayla nods.

"What you don't know is that she came after me for interrupting their taunts. She and Alex both--" Kelly continues, looking down.

"What happened?"

"Alex…he--" Kelly stops speaking. "I'm *not* that confident person you believe me to be…"

"*What* happened?" Kayla repeats, now leaning forward.

"She goaded him and--"

"What!"

Kelly looks up sharply at her friend because of the high pitch in her voice.

"He was--"

"I think I know what you're saying, Kelly. Does anyone know?"

"Just you…"

"Is *that* the reason why you want to go to Australia? To get away from all this…" Kayla blurts out. "It sounds like you need these meds yourself…"

"I don't want to be on meds. Especially not now I know how badly they affect you…"

Kayla grabs her phone, and after a few motions, she holds it up.

"What's that?" Kelly asks.

"It's something that's been happening lately called 'me too'... Well, that's what it's being referred. It's for people like you to feel safe. If I'm right about what happened to you, you should post this on your profile on Facebook and other places and make certain people know about what happened. Not hide it and let them get away with it..." Kayla explains. "And if I'd known about you, I would never have had him as my boyfriend..."

"It's the past. It cannot be changed. I'm not planning to dwell on it," Kelly states. "I was struggling with whether to tell you, but then you told me what he and Lisa did to you. When you told me that I knew I had to tell you this. But it was hard to tell you nonetheless..."

"I can imagine it was. But as you say, it's the past. But--"

"But...?" Kelly gives her friend a confused stare.

"I need some time to think it over. It's kind of hard to deal with knowing what happened," Kayla states softly. "I need a bit of time to process it."

"I've bottled this up so long and--" Kelly wails.

"I guess I know *why*. Now everything makes sense, and why they'd be together. Well, I guess they deserve one another after how they acted towards you," Kayla snaps angrily. "In fact, I'm angrier at what they did to *you* than anything done to me…"

"So, you're not angry with me?"

"Why should I be? It wasn't your fault. You said it wasn't my fault, but the same goes for *you*. Even more so…"

Kelly nods, then she looks down.

"And Kelly, in a way, you've made it easier for *me* to move on from it. Before you told me this, a small part of me wanted to forgive him, and try to win him back. But not now…"

"I didn't have medication to help me cope as you have," Kelly whispers.

She sighs before adding, "It's easier for me to say you can get better than for me to say to same about myself. I'm supposed to be popular, happy and have all these friends but when I'm sitting in the middle of a crowd, I often feel the loneliest, especially when you're not there…"

"Kelly, look at me."

Kelly hesitates then glances up at her friend.

"You've always been there for me, and you know that," Kayla continues. "I think we both made mistakes with us hiding these things from one another. But today that ends. No more secrets ever…okay?"

Kelly nods shallowly then looks down again, but a moment later looks up. "What do we do until then? I don't want anyone to know I'm leaving…"

"I'll think of something."

"Like what?"

"I don't know. I have to think about it, okay," Kayla snaps somewhat forcefully, then adds in a gentler voice. "I won't tell any of what we talked about. It's our secret."

"I don't want anyone to know about the chemo…"

"I respect your wishes about it. But finding out was hard really," Kayla says quietly. "I have these images going through my mind about how you might end up looking. I've seen the pictures in the news…"

"The doctor says it isn't something most people die of. The treatment is getting better all the time…" Kelly sighs again deeply.

"I guess my plans for my life are totally different now…" she adds after a few minutes go by silently.

"I'm guessing that things are *more* similar for us than either of us wants to admit, Kelly."

Kelly nods curtly.

"Both of us kept things hidden too well for either of us to notice of the other person" Kayla continues. "I hid my depression and what happened at home from you and if you hadn't pushed me into telling you I probably wouldn't have told you about Alex, and then you'd still be guilt-tripping yourself over what he did to you."

Another nod.

"It wasn't your fault ever, okay…" Kayla is about to continue speaking when she's interrupted, and her friend's words cause her to slump back, feeling renewed shock because they now make her suspicions about what was going even more real and confirm she'd started to suspect--he'd never loved her.

"He raped me. It was about ten years ago…"

Chapter 14

KAYLA LOOKS DOWN, FEELING DEFLATED by her friend's admission.

It's now out about what Kelly has been hiding.

It's clear to her that it's likely even more painful than anything she's endured herself. In the process of them discussing a growing rift between them as friends, it has become clear that the words spoken during their first meeting at the doctor's office didn't count for much.

It was Kayla's idea back then they'd never keep secrets.

Now, it's so obvious that both did the very opposite of their promise to one another.

Their behaviour had been caused by things they'd interpreted as something the other person would consider shameful somehow, even though it showed now that it was never true and that it had always just been them forcefully hiding stuff from one another.

I'm not even certain if it was a possible lack of trust that caused us to behave this way towards one another. Maybe it was something else. It could be we picked up this behaviour from social media or the news or something.

It's obvious now to Kayla how important her next words will be for Kelly. She sighs deeply, then turns to her friend and speaks, "Kelly, I told you what's up with me. The girl *you* saw standing at the door this morning--"

Kayla stops a moment before she continues, speaking quietly. "That's *not* me, really. Most days I can't cope with people. I prefer being alone…"

"So that's the real reason why you never visit *me* is because you're--" Kelly begins to say.

"People generally don't react well whenever a person tells them they're depressed," Kayla interjects hastily.

Another pause and then Kayla shows her bluntness from earlier in the day, "If *every* time someone I told to 'get over it', and it gave me a stack of banknotes to pay my bills for a week, I might have been able to live rent-free, with no uni bills, and no other bills…it just seems that people never value whenever someone deals with something that impacts their life, their health, their state of mind."

"I guess I need to tell you why I haven't been in

touch…" Kelly whispers.

"I kind of guessed it when you said about the chemo. And that other thing--" Kayla breaths deeply. "The fact you were raped. Maybe you're depressed because of that. We promised each other never to keep secrets from one another. It's about time we start to obey our rule…"

"I agree. I just don't know if I can bring myself to tell you what's up with me," Kelly suggests softly. "If as you say it's because I'm depressed…"

"Just take your time. I'll wait however long it takes you. I know something about how you're feeling and what is going on with you. Those words confirm it. I'll wait…"

Kelly looks down for a moment then she nods curtly.

~~~

KELLY STARES AT THE PAINTING ABOVE THE SOFA and considers her words carefully. She had already mentioned about cancer, but now the tougher subject had to be discussed. She isn't sure how her friend would react to it.

"I don't think it's good to keep secrets. It's what my parents are doing. We shouldn't be doing the same. We're better people than that…" Kayla almost whispers the words because she's now fearful that her friend would
~~~

become angry but when no angry response comes, she continues even more softly.

"But we *both* need to find a way to deal with what we had to go through. We did it alone for *too* long. We were keeping it hidden even from each other. Maybe…"

"I think that the best thing is for us to go away. To move to Australia," Kelly says quietly, then sighing before adding, "To start over without any hassles or jerks around."

"I agree…"

"I've done some of the preparations already and told Auntie Josie I was going to speak with you about whether you wanted to come. If it's a definite 'yes' from you then I need to call her to tell her that we're interested. She had said I had to be quick about it…"

"Why is that?"

"She said she needed to know because if we just turned up, they could be on the road already. In the first few days she could drive back home to meet up with us and then take us with her," Kelly explains. "But later on, we would have to find our own accommodation until she got back home."

"I would guess she's travelling quite far from her home by the sound of that," Kayla suggests, "It makes sense for her not to want to have to keep travelling back, or for us to turn up with her gone…"

"The treatment is for three months. Her tour is going to be for four months…" Kelly continues. "Let me think. She said she's going in six weeks' time. The means she'll be long gone whenever we can go."

"So, we go in six months from now," Kayla suggests next. "Three months for you to get your treatment, and then, while you're doing that, I'll get a job in the same town to pay for both our bills."

"Are you okay with that idea? Would you be able to cope?"

"Yeah…errr…yeah, I think so. Yes, I will male myself cope."

"Okay, I guess I'll have to call Auntie Josie later…"

Kayla nods.

Kelly looks at her friend for a time before returning to her pensive mood. She stares out of the window at the field beyond that, in that very moment, decides to get bathed in bright sunlight. She smiles ever so slightly.

I guess she wanted to go out to process the news. But there's a chance I scared her off with my announcement about having cancer…or even my admission about Alex. Maybe I should never have mentioned that. She sounded really upset when she heard it. But if she's right about that stuff she said about people telling more and more about when something like that it was maybe best for me to have mentioned. Hiding it away is not good for me. I've done it for too long.

"Kayla, you said you needed time to process my announcement. Do you need to?"

"I was just contemplating it," Kayla responds. "I think it would help to figure out about Australia and everything else…Do you mind it if I go off for a walk to think about it all?"

"That's why I asked. I think it will do you some good to be out in the fresh air," Kelly says, waving her hands towards the doorway.

Kayla nods, then she gathers all her belongings into her bag, and is greeted by Kelly's giggle when the book with the erotica story is among the belongings packed.

"You said I could borrow it…"

"Of course, go ahead. Just don't let them see you with that…" Kelly points towards Kayla's bag. "I think they'd get even more wrong ideas about us then…"

Chapter 15

Kayla LOOKS OUT OF THE DOOR TO SEE if the men are close to the houses and seeing them walking away in the distance and then turning the corner going out of view.

She slams the door shut behind her, cringing somewhat when it echoes, then starts walking into the opposite direction to where the men had gone.

I guess I'm nervous now because of my earlier behaviour. I guess I'll have to say sorry to Kelly about it properly. I hope she's okay in there...

She glances behind her to make certain the street is still empty. She sees no one.

"I guess I can go to the coffee shop without Kelly," Kayla mutters. "I guess I'll get questions about turning up alone but as Kelly says I have to take more responsibility for how I feel..."

She starts walking briskly.

Suddenly, she wants to be somewhere indoors.

Suddenly 'being outside' feels uncomfortable. She feels that familiar feeling of tightness in her chest that happens every time when she feels a panic.

She pulls her bag closer, and then is about to reach inside it for her medication, but then stops in mid-motion.

"No, I'm doing what Kelly said to do. This is the day when I'm not taking them."

She glances around her again, then she breathes in a few times to calm herself, then slows her pace to a slow, almost leisurely so anyone seeing her would just see someone on a leisurely walk.

Her destination is the coffee shop that's just a few streets from Kelly's home.

While she walks, she thinks about her conversation with her friend. It had been awash with hidden truth about them both proving that they hadn't been as close in recent years as they both had been convincing themselves.

The conversation had been a charged back-and-forth of revealing information that wasn't known by the other person.

"We kept so much hidden…" Kayla mumbles. "But why? That's not how real friends should behave…"

She turns a corner and then crosses the street. Now she walks faster because she feels spots of rain on her face. She almost runs the last hundred yards to the coffee shop instinctively.

She stops in front of the shop next to it to check that her makeup isn't all streaked in every direction, then, with a few brisk steps, she's at the door and walks inside.

"Hey there, Kayla, isn't Kelly with you today?"

"No, sorry, what…errr…no she isn't. She wasn't feeling well so sent me to get some food for us."

Kayla hopes her face isn't bright red and that the man serving the food, going by the name Jake doesn't notice her pensive mood or that she's not quite being truthful. She smiles at him, distracted.

"I guess the usual?" he asks.

"Yes, please. And a large coffee for me please…"

"The 'usual' mixed salads for you both, right?"

"Errr…yes, please. Is Mandy around? I want to ask her something."

"Yeah, she's upstairs with the baby. Let me call her to let her know you're here."

"Thanks."

Kayla watches Jake walk to a small room at the back of the coffee shop, then cringes when his voice booms the message up the stairs she knows to be there. A few moments later, she hears the voice of Mandy calling back.

"She's just dealing with his nappy. She'll bring him down with her in a minute, then you can have some time to talk with her and play with the baby at the same time," Jake says when he's back in front on Kayla. "So, how's uni?"

"Just a few more classes left this semester, then…as they say…school's out."

"Ah, right, and what's planned for the summer?"

"Nothing much. Got a new job lined up I might take."

"I told you long ago that retail isn't the sort of right work for you…"

"I guess you're right. I guess I found out it wasn't right for me way too late."

"Still not interested in catering, huh?" Jake asks as he

packs the boxes of salad into a small bag. "I can give you a job here for lunchtime work…"

"I'll think about it…"

"Ah, a better answer than last time when you outright dismissed it as ridiculous. What's changed?"

"I guess I've had an epiphany…"

Kayla grins when Jake laughs loud, then, as Mandy walks into the shop he calls out at her, "It seems it took an epiphany for her give my suggestion a consideration."

"I told you that she'd tell you if she's interested," Mandy calls out. "But I know her too well. And that didn't sound at all like she was saying yes."

"So, still not a yes, then?" Jake asks, turning to Kayla.

"Okay, a maybe, alright. But only if you stop bitching at me about it."

"Fair enough."

~~~

Kayla glances past Mandy towards Jake and frowns a moment when he winks at her. She glances at Mandy who grins at her.
~~~

"Don't mind him. He always tries to flirt with every girl who walks into the shop," Mandy says. "But he does know about Alex because he overheard some girls talk about him when I was shopping at the shopping mall with this fuzz ball here…"

"What was said?"

"Not much really. He listened to them, then told me. If that's what you wanted to talk to me about, I already know about it," Mandy says. She takes hold of Kayla's hand. "Remember what I said to you about him. I told you that I wasn't sure about his sincerity… Does Kelly know what happened…?"

"Yeah, she knows. I told her today," Kayla answers. "Also told her about Lisa…"

"She told me she's going away in a few months," Mandy continues. "I asked her if you knew. She said she was going to talk to you about it."

"She did. I'm going with her…" Kayla whispers. "That's why I couldn't tell Jake I'd take the job…"

Mandy glances over her shoulder before she leans forward then whispers conspiratorially, "I'll tell him after you're gone, okay… But the fuzz ball here will miss his favourite babysitter. That I'm sure of…"

"I'll miss him too… Is he on solids yet?

"Not quite yet. But he has settled into a decent sleep pattern that makes it easier for Jake and I to get enough sleep," Mandy says, grinning broadly. "I guess I'll need a new babysitter, and Jake will need to plead with other people walking in if they're interested in a job here. We're getting rather busy now. I guess I was proved wrong about the success of this place…"

"I hope this place does become really successful…" Kayla says, smiling broadly.

"So do I…" Mandy says, but then she seems to want to talk about the real reason why Kayla had asked for her.

"Did you ask Kelly about what happened to her?"

Chapter 16

KAYLA LOOKS AT MANDY INCREDULOUSLY. How did she know about Kelly when she didn't? She frowns, and for a moment, feels an uncommon anger well up inside her towards Kelly for confiding in someone else other than her own best friend.

"I know about it because one morning I was serving here instead of Jake, and she was sitting on the bench in the corner behind you…" Mandy says softly. "She told me about both things, though I saw she was struggling… You have told her finally about your depression, right?"

Kayla nods after a moment of hesitation, then suddenly realises that for the last six years, Mandy had been a friend for both and that she was probably the reason why there was even a friendship between them still.

Without Mandy's gentle nudges Kelly and she would have fallen out and parted ways a long time ago.

The reason she visited Kelly wasn't down to her mom telling her to get out of bed.

It was more down to Mandy telling a few days earlier to go visit Kelly, and she'd promised to do this.

"Kelly is going to need you. She can't have stress or upset because that might make recovery tough on her body…"

Another glance from Mandy towards Jake, then she turns and continues speaking.

"Jake is taking it hard. His grandma died of cancer. He held his tears in while she was here, but then after Kelly left, I found him in the corner in the back room crying," Mandy explains. "He wants to play the tough guy usually, but deep down, he's really sensitive. Especially when it comes to this topic…"

"Do you know about Kelly's aunt?"

"She told me about her aunt when she heard about Jake's grandma," Mandy answers.

"I promised not to tell, but it seems Kelly has similar cancer as her aunt…" Kayla says.

"That means it won't be deadly," Mandy whispers. "I checked it up. Twenty years ago, a lot of people could die from it, but now it's less than five per cent who even are ill from it long term. And even fewer die…"

"Oh, right. I guess I should read up on it," Kayla says.

"If you're going to go with Kelly and therefore be caring for her while she's recovering then I would say it's best to know as much as you can..." Mandy says. "But that will be easy with your degree... Congrats on passing your exams, by the way."

Kayla smiles at Mandy before she speaks once more, "It seems Kelly and I are going to work on a book about her treatment and about my depression. We're even working on getting me to rely less on the tablets I'm on..."

"Good. That's going to be tough. I hope you do realise that."

Kayla nods curtly.

"I'm not stopping them immediately. Kelly suggested I skip one day each week at first," she explains. "Then once every six days, then every five days and so on. Or something like it. It's Kelly's idea, so I'll go by what she says to do."

"Being positive also helps..."

"Kelly said that too..."

"I thought as much," Mandy says. "She's always

looking out for other people's well-being before her own."

"I mistook it as her being popular," Kayla says shyly. "But now I see she just does it because it's the nice thing to do…"

Mandy squeezes Kayla's hand tighter, then a moment later, their attention is diverted by them both cooing Mandy's baby who had woken up and was making it known to the two women talking that he was after some attention from them now.

"I'll send you presents from Australia. Maybe a giant koala bear toy for him…"

Kayla nods at Mandy's baby.

"He would love that very much…" Mandy responds. "I still am so happy I chose the name you suggested for him. It's a nice name…"

"I guess Wyatt won't remember me…" Kayla says before chuckling a bit. "Does Jake know it's a character from Charmed?"

"I tried to explain it to him, but as he has never seen the programme, it goes right over his head," Mandy says, laughing. "Unless *stuff* suddenly starts flying around, he'll never accept the name is from the show…"

They both laugh, then stare at Jake who shrugs a

"what's going on?" back at them.

"So, when are you two leaving?"

"Not decided yet," Kayla answers quietly. "Her aunt is doing some sort of show to promote her ranch's work. We have until…let's see, it would be four months from now to turn up. But the treatment starts in three weeks' time and takes three months."

"I think it's best Kelly does that and only travel after she's stronger…So wait until after her aunt is back home," Mandy suggests.

"I think that's the plan," Kayla states, then she pauses and stares towards Jake again. "Perhaps I should come to work here for a few days a week. Kelly says that doing things differently will help me with my depression. And no, don't tell him yet. I need a bit of time to think it over and to work out how Kelly and I are going to do things in general…"

"It sounds like you and Kelly did a lot of soul-searching if you have been talking lately…" Mandy suggests.

"I was at her house today. We talked all morning and some of this afternoon too, "Kayla states. "I was actually rather shocked to hear about her cancer. I said I needed some time to think…"

"As in 'go visit Mandy and have a heart to heart talk

with the only person who understands me' and her to figure out what to do…" Mandy quips, grinning broadly. "I'm a friend of both of you. I've seen the two of you grow up from teenagers to two smart women over the last decade, and have you both visit me regularly for advice and pep talks…"

"I appreciate the pep talks…"

"I will be here for these chats for as long as both of you are still here," Mandy says. "And a ranch…hmm… perhaps, if things go well enough, we can save up to come to Australia for a vacation, but that would be several years in the future. I make a promise we'll try to come to visit you both if we can save up enough… okay?"

Mandy is answered by a broad happy smile.

"I'll talk with Jake and suggest to him you've told me you want to work…How many days you'd want a job for?"

"How much is the job paying? Sorry to ask. I have bills to pay. Maybe not as many if I'm crashing on the spare bed at Kelly's house now…"

"Hang on. Let me go check…if that's okay?"

Kayla nods, then she feels a pang of panic again as she watches Mandy speaking to Jake, and sees him look at her, but then when his expression becomes compassionate, she realises that he always wanted to be kind to her too…

Chapter 17

KAYLA LOOKS AROUND THE CORNER TO SEE if the workmen are present in the street just outside Kelly's house.

"Dammit, I guess I'll have to go past them to get to her house," she hisses under her breath, almost like she must give voice to her own earlier behaviour. "I guess my behaviour this morning was stupid."

After being away for most of the remainder of the afternoon, talking to Mandy and later also gingerly striking up a conversation with Jake about his grandmother, Kayla had hoped that the workmen would be gone for the day. But they were not.

She curses, then straightens up and thinks deeply over her options.

I promised Kelly I'd be back today...Dammit.

She glances around and walks the alleyway between

the gardens. She sees a man in the distance so decides against the idea that popped into her head.

He'd think I'm some cat burglar…

Kayla turns and somewhat in a deflated mood walks back to the corner of the street. She stands there, staring aimlessly towards the other end of the street.

Panic sets in when, looking around the corner, she sees that the workmen are back at their earlier spot where they'd called after her as she walked past.

She breathes in, and then again.

"You can do this, girl," she mumbles, "Just ignore them and walk past them pretending not to notice they're there…this time."

She starts walking. At first, the pace is hesitant and slow, but as she gets closer to where she can turn right into the front garden of Kelly's home, her pace quickens. She decides against running, and instead, measures her pace against the heart beats she feels pounding against her chest.

Her hand tightens around the bag handle of the bag with the two salads inside it, and she presses her handbag tightly against her waist.

She hears the first whistle from one of the men. She fights the urge to do what she'd done before.

No! If I do that then Kelly will be annoyed and tell me to go and never come back. I might then not be allowed to come with her for the trip…

She knocks firmly on the front door and waits, now feeling pensive and drawn inward even more than earlier. She listens at the same time for footsteps within the house…

~~~

KELLY LOOKS UP WITH SHE HEARS A SOFT KNOCK on the front door, then it repeats a few more times. She glances for a moment at the clock on the wall. It's almost five in the afternoon.

She gets up and walks to the window and, as had happened earlier in the day, she sees Kayla standing outside.

However, this time she's silent, almost pensive and seeming drawn inward with the mind on something other than paying attention to the men whistling and catcalling at her.

Kelly puts her mug down in the sink, and rushes to the front door and opens it quickly.

"So, what are the plans, then? Have you decided when to go?" Kayla asks, and she looks at her friend before she enters the house once more, then hearing
~~~

footsteps she almost dives into the house in a panic, evoking a momentary grin from her friend.

Kelly shuts the door behind her and looks at her friend to assess what mood she might be in. She sees Kayla's eyes glazed over.

"I guess it wasn't pleasant going past them after how you acted towards them earlier," Kelly says softly.

Kayla shakes her head but not because she's annoyed. In fact, Kayla's behaviour leaves her in awe of her friend and some level of renewed respect too.

"Can I ask why you returned?" she asks gently.

Kayla hesitates a moment before answering the question, "I thought it all over. Also decided to talk with Mandy as well. I especially thought it over because of what I had said this morning to you. In a way, it made me realise how stupid it is for me to try to pretend to be something I'm *not*."

"And that is?"

Kelly keeps her tone gentle.

"I guess…a bitch," Kayla says bitterly. "Especially not when I should consider you. You matter *too* much to me."

"I think I acted like a bitch *too*, thinking I'm the only

one with problems," Kelly responds. "I ignored what mom always says. She told me this last year and said that when you're having a problem *also* to look around you as it will show you that others have them *too*. I guess this stuff going on with me, has taught me not to make everything just about me."

"I shouldn't have said that you are being smart or pretty makes you a bad person," Kayla admits. "I didn't see how unhappy you really are, but I see it now…"

"I didn't see it either with you and that's what annoys me about me the most. I want things to be right between us."

"Me too," Kayla comments. "I think we need to rethink how we treat each other every day of our lives now."

"Let's sit down, and let's make decisions about what we're going to do next…okay?"

Kayla nods.

Kelly, with her friend closely following her, walk single file back into her living room.

They sit down at the same time side by side on the sofa, both flopping back against the six massive cushions and then both sighing deeply.

A smile appears on each of their faces when each

realises how matched their reactions really are because of their lifelong friendship, then both look forward again, both feeling pensive once more...

Chapter 18

Kelly and Kayla stare at one another for a while silently, then Kayla takes hold of Kelly's hand.

She sighs, which causes Kelly to flash a gentle smile back at her.

"I think I've decided that I *want* to come with you. If you're going to go through chemo, you cannot do it on your own. I *know* I have my own battles to fight, but I think that as friends *we* can make things easier."

"What about the family? Uni? All our friends?"

"Your health is more important. We just pack up and *go*. Never again will we hide *who* we are from each other, okay?"

"Okay."

"When do we leave?"

"I'm all packed up already. Have been packed up for three weeks. Get your stuff from home, and when you're back we get going," Kelly answers. "And no, I won't suddenly leave and allow you to be left stranded."

"Okay."

"I guess 'K and K' are going to be the new Thelma and Louise in a way…" Kelly says with a chuckle escaping her lips.

She smiles before adding in a more teasing voice, "With a peppering of Bonnie and Clyde. I guess you, with your short hair, can be Clyde…"

"I'll pack all my classic clothing in my case," Kayla grins for a moment. "I doubt we can get away with robbing banks and stores, though."

"Actually, I had a different idea just now."

"Which is?" Kayla's face fills now with curiosity.

"Why don't you write a journal about all this. We can get it published later, and then it may even help others."

"Maybe, it should be some sort of story, telling everyone about your how you coped with living with your cancer and then living with having the chemo. In my case, it can be about how it feels to have had depression since my childhood and afterwards," Kayla states softly. "I guess I kept my depression *too* well hidden from everyone. Even from you, especially from you. Will you forgive me for that...?"

"We'll publish, and it list 'K and K' on the cover, and--" Kelly replies. "And of course, we have to *do* this. We're friends after all. Friends forgive each other. I do think people will wonder who, or what, K and K are..."

"Good idea. And everyone who reads the book should tell others to buy the book too. Maybe we'll live a decent enough life in the end. Any other ideas for books?" Kayla says. "I guess it was tougher for you to decide whether to tell me as you could die..."

"I was told that a few years of chemo can fix stuff. I'm not worried about it. I was more worried about how you'd react or how to tell you," Kelly explains. "When I mentioned Auntie Josie earlier, did you actually remember her?"

"The crazy chick who went off to live in Australia? You always called her that when we were children..."

"Yes, she's one and I think I told you about her years ago. She knows about me, about what's going on with me right now. When I spoke with her a week or so ago, she told me *she* had cancer three decades ago," Kelly explains.

Kelly pauses for a moment then she adds more information.

"I'm the only one in the whole family who knows about it. She told me she'll keep it secret about *me* if I do the same about her. She told me that my mom would freak out if she knows about either us having this cancer, or about the fact that she had it twenty years ago. That's another reason, besides other reason previously mentioned, *why* I just want to…why I want to just leave."

"I guess I understand now. In a way, I was doing the same by staying in my house most days and drawing my curtains."

"In my case, I guessed I favoured the silence," Kelly states. "But now, go get all your stuff you're bringing with you when we leave. Then we'll leave when the time is right--"

Kayla turns, and she rushes off, glancing back once to be met with a reassuring nod like the one she'd received in the past whenever Kelly had felt the need to be encouraging…

~~~

KELLY GRINS A MOMENT WHEN SHE HEARS KAYLA snap a swear word at one of the men outside, who'd obviously decided to react to her rushing past once more, but now the volley of curse words coming from Kayla is almost comical now.

"I guess she did that behaviour to give herself something hide behind. It's probably all pretence… I
~~~

doubt she enjoys swearing."

Kelly looks in the mirror for a moment before she sits down. Now she just must wait for her friend's return.

She looks in her mug, then shrugs, and feels remorse for all the months of avoiding her best friend.

She of all people would understand, and today's conversation proved it beyond a doubt.

"So, you just wanted to be hidden from everyone, stupid girl," Kelly murmurs at her reflection, staring in the mirror intently and appraising her features for several moments. She turns around in a circle a few times then she nods.

"Why not flaunt it instead. As Auntie Josie says… there are *other* ways to be beautiful," Kelly murmurs once more, now smiling. "Maybe I just was scared. But what Auntie Josie also said, is that I don't need to fear any of *this*. She's alive and has been free of her cancer for more than fifteen years. She has a ten-year-old son, too. He was born after she received the news that she was in remission. So, why do I hide…?"

Kelly gets up again, then walks across the room to her handbag and grabs her phone from it.

After a few minutes checking the listings, she finds the number she wants.

She dials it, and after a pause to wait for someone to answer it, she speaks, "Hiya, Auntie Josie, is the offer of visiting *you* still on the table?"

THE END

Here's how to keep in touch with me!

My website is **www.nathaliemlromer.com**

Twitter   twitter.com/nmlromer
Facebook   facebook.com/nathaliemlromer
Blog   nathaliemlromer.blog
GoodReads goodreads.com/nathaliemlromer
Bookbub   bookbub.com/authors/nathalie-m-l-romer

"Thank you so much for reading my book. I hope
it will give you many more years of enjoyment."

Nathalie M.L. Römer

Hidden: One title. Endless Possibilities.

From scifi to romance, fantasy to cozy mystery & many more, the *Hidden Project* has something for everyone.

Each author has taken the same title, and put their own spin on the story, leading to a wide range of stories in a variety of genres.

You can check out all the books in the *Hidden Project* here:

HiddenReader.com

Or join us on

Facebook facebook.com/hiddenreader

or

subscribe to our newsletter eepurl.com/cHr3Q1

My Own Story With Depression…

My battle with depression started when was in my early teens, and continued throughout my life.

Like Kayla in the story I had to cope with being bullied, but unlike her I didn't take medication.

Later in life I was battling with PTSD and anxiety because of other reasons that I won't list here.

Life's tough, and often an uphill battle to have a normal day. The feelings associated with this are deep inside me, deep in a place that no one else but me knows it exists. Life is hard to deal with for someone who has depression.

Generally, with this illness, you feel more vulnerable, you feel more sensitive to criticism, and you're affected physically by the symptoms. It's not an illness that just in someone's mind.

You also can feel physically sick, and to me the feelings are almost like flu (the closest comparison I can give).

If you know someone and he or she says they are depressed I would take it seriously. Tell *them* to seek medical help. The initial treatment with medication can often make life more bearable later on.

I manage my depression with the general guidelines associated with art therapy but this isn't for everyone. I'm not a medical expert in any way and I've gone with a treatment that works for me. Listen to the doctor and follow their advice.

But foremost, if you know a person who has depression, or anxiety, or any of the associated illnesses the knowledge that they are being believed is often the first positive step in managing the illness and overcoming it.

Just like an apple a day keeps the doctor away, a kind word keeps the mind from sinking into a dark place.

Don't ever ignore mental illness, neither in terms of how it affects a person nor in the reasoning that somehow it's a made up illness in someone's head. It isn't. Never tell a person to get over it because that's not possible.

Some people will go through a life time battling this disease without ever overcoming it.

It's real.

It can be devastating for a person. It can control their daily life. Be that person they can rely on when their day is at its darkest. So show support through compassion, listening without judgement and by showing in general that you care.

My life is okay now. My partner Anders knows how I

feel in general and he always offers me a shoulder to cry on when days are bad for me.

I'm working on my recovery for the severe depression I was diagnosed with in 2007, and chose to treat it without the medication. My doctor was okay with that but warned me that if my symptoms didn't improve I would need medication.

I discovered about art therapy, adopting the guidelines as a way to manage my illness. I'm naturally artistic so was capable of expressing my feelings pretty easily in digital drawing I'd do.

Then, in November 2014, I realised I could try my hand at writing. Initially it was slow work. I made a lot of mistakes, partly because the stress involved with this industry can be tough.

You need to be able to walk away with chin up if someone says your writing is crap…for example.

But after a time, with the advice from several people, one of them being author Orna Ross, I started to realise that I'm writing for **me** foremost. If I put more of me into a story, I was realising, I could create stories that were charged with the same emotions I might feel on any given day.

From a few comments I've received since, I'm apparently creating characters with "good characterisation who have depth of emotion and who aren't people afraid to be angry, sad, happy, annoyed, etc.".

I guess I'm learning to recognise that the characters in my stories need to come over as real people. And a real person deals every day with a myriad of emotions.

By putting those emotions into my writing I've found a way to unload some of the emotions associated with being depressed, and therefore I started to have more better days in general.

But life will keep being tough until I'm recovered from the depression which the doctor stated could take a decade or more.

But I'm a positive person by nature, and see things generally with the "glass half full". Even days that were the worst in my life I would look at life in that way. Perhaps it is that which stops me from sliding down again.

So now I've written this story.

A story that's emotionally charged for me in terms of writing it. The references about depression are a direct reference to how I've felt over the years. The remaining details are fictional except for the references made about Auntie Josie and her son.

I knew a woman in around 2003. She was in remission when I knew her. Like Auntie Josie she had cancer about two decades earlier that had started in her mid-twenties.

HIDDEN

She went into remission and a decade into her remission she gave birth to a healthy baby boy. He's around 27 or 28 years old now if I remember his age correctly.

I don't recall the type of cancer she had but I do remember this story because she told me it and I was amazed about it.

That's my message of hope to each and every person out there who suffers from cancer, and I wish all those who have it or are recovering from it to have a speedy and full recovery.

So, in short, my story is about hope. About the fact life can and will always get better if you do something about it. I'm not hiding my depression from anyone, and neither should you if that's what you deal with.

And tell a person who told you they're dealing with it that talking about is the first step in their own recovery…

Be Strong and Blessed Be,

Nathalie M.L. Römer
Author and Publisher

ABOUT THE AUTHOR

Nathalie M.L. Römer was born in the Netherlands, lived there during childhood before she moved to Curaçao as a teenager. From there, she then moved to Britain to live there for twenty-five years, before moving to Sweden where she now lives with her partner Anders.

In her childhood years and beyond, Nathalie has always loved to read novels. In her local library as a child, she would often borrow "adult audience" science fiction and fantasy novels, and as the book worm, that she was (and still is), would read them all in a few days...and go back for more, often. The genres that interest Nathalie the most is science fiction, fantasy and historical novels. Her favourite authors include various science fiction, fantasy and historic authors that include (but are not limited to) Isaac Asimov, Richard A. Knaak, Jean M. Auel, and Christie Golden.

In addition, to reading novels, the other interests she pursues include needlework and crafts, archaeology, various science topics, home cooking, photography, web design, and playing MMO games - mostly World of Warcraft which Nathalie credits as having directly inspired her to start writing stories. She plays on the World of Warcraft EU server Shadowsong.